Sai Baba lived in India in a village named Shirdi and touched many hearts with his love and compassion. He loved and was loved unconditionally. People came to Sai Baba with life-threatening problems, and he gave them hope and healing. He was known as a repository of wisdom. Rich and poor were the same to Baba. He spoke with love and kindness. The stories and teachings of Baba bring peace and happiness to the listener.

A Loving Saint: Sai Baba has been blessed in the Samadhi Mandir in Shirdi. May this book bless your home as well.

www.mascotbooks.com

A Loving Saint: Sai Baba

©2019 Arthi Gokarn. All Rights Reserved. No part of this publication may be reproduced, stored in a retrieval system or transmitted in any form by any means electronic, mechanical, or photocopying, recording or otherwise without the permission of the author.

For more information, please contact:
Mascot Books
620 Herndon Parkway, Suite 320
Herndon, VA 20170
info@mascotbooks.com

Library of Congress Control Number: 2019901283

CPSIA Code: PRT0619A
ISBN-13: 978-1-64307-422-1

Printed in the United States

A LOVING SAINT

SAI BABA

written by
Arthi Gokarn

illustrated by
David Flenniken & Arthi Gokarn

Once upon a time, a little boy was born in India. He was abandoned at birth. However, he was discovered and adopted by foster parents who were very loving and kind.

They were thrilled to have this little boy called Baba in their life and thought of him as a gift from God.

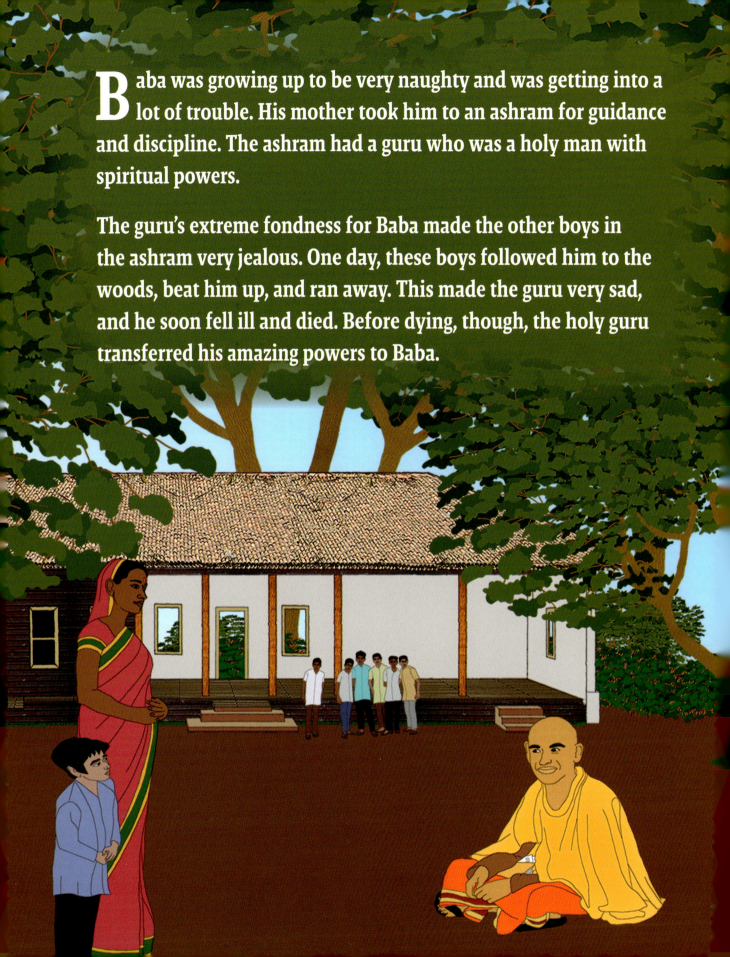

Baba was growing up to be very naughty and was getting into a lot of trouble. His mother took him to an ashram for guidance and discipline. The ashram had a guru who was a holy man with spiritual powers.

The guru's extreme fondness for Baba made the other boys in the ashram very jealous. One day, these boys followed him to the woods, beat him up, and ran away. This made the guru very sad, and he soon fell ill and died. Before dying, though, the holy guru transferred his amazing powers to Baba.

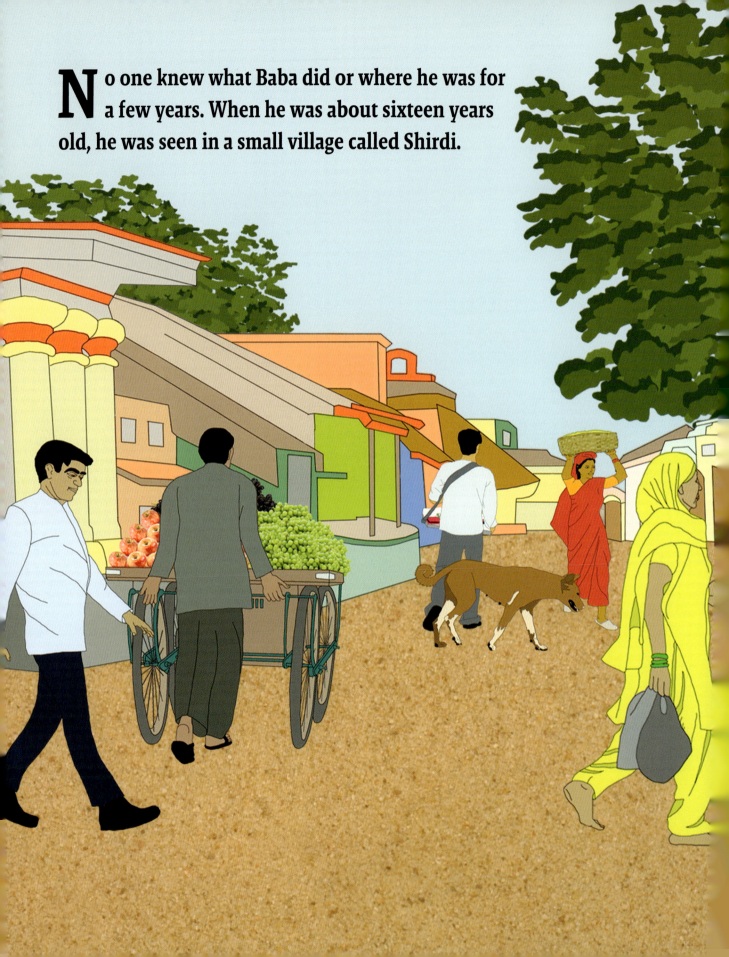

No one knew what Baba did or where he was for a few years. When he was about sixteen years old, he was seen in a small village called Shirdi.

He lived a very simple life, like that of a monk. The people of Shirdi were surprised to see such a young boy meditating for hours under a neem tree.

He left Shirdi only to return with a marriage party a few years later. He was then called "Sai Baba" by the people in Shirdi.

One day, a man named Shama was bitten by a poisonous snake. The poison was spreading rapidly through his body and he was going to die, but Baba miraculously cured him. This news of the miraculous cure spread like wildfire throughout the village.

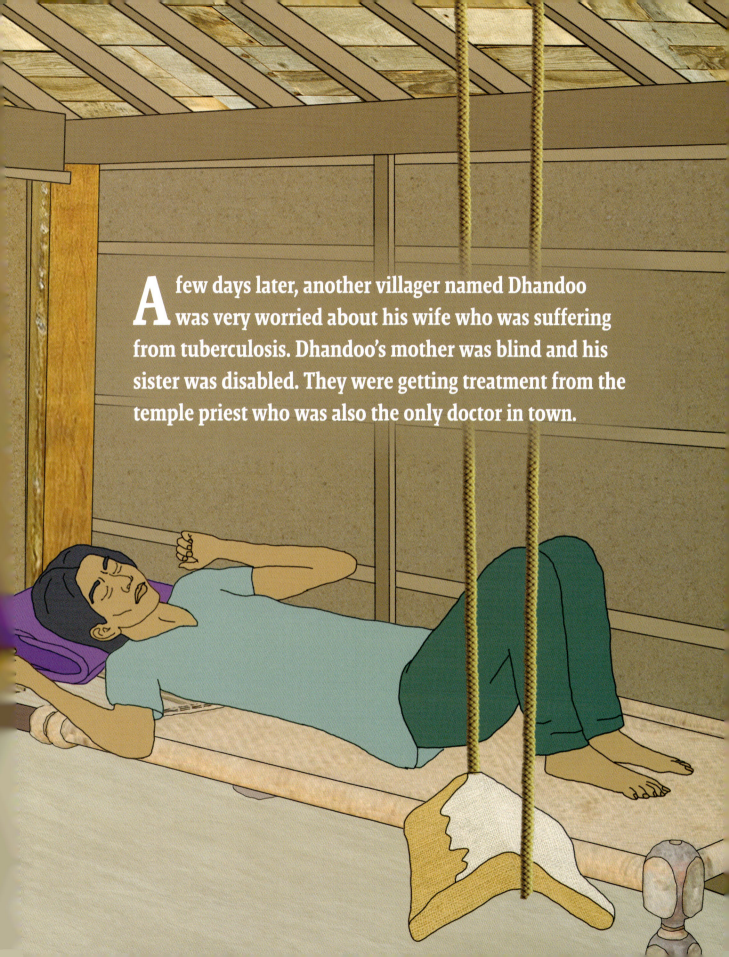

A few days later, another villager named Dhandoo was very worried about his wife who was suffering from tuberculosis. Dhandoo's mother was blind and his sister was disabled. They were getting treatment from the temple priest who was also the only doctor in town.

Dhandoo excitedly told the temple priest about Baba's miraculous cure of the snake bite. This made the priest very jealous and angry. He was afraid this Baba would take his patients away. In a fit of rage, he denied further treatment to all members of Dhandoo's family.

Dhandoo begged the priest for forgiveness, but the priest's words were set in stone. Dhandoo was never again allowed to set foot in the temple.

Dhandoo lost all hope for his wife, mother, and sister to recover. He felt miserable. He deeply regretted having spoken of the wondrous cures of Sai Baba. Now his family suffered, all because of him.

When Dhandoo reached home that evening, his wife's condition had worsened. She could barely breathe and needed immediate medical help.

Because the priest had refused to treat his family, Dhandoo ran to Baba. The saint greeted Dhandoo with love and consoled him. He gave Dhandoo hope that his family would recover.

Sai Baba gave Dhandoo some holy ash. "This can cure your whole family of all their ailments," he said.

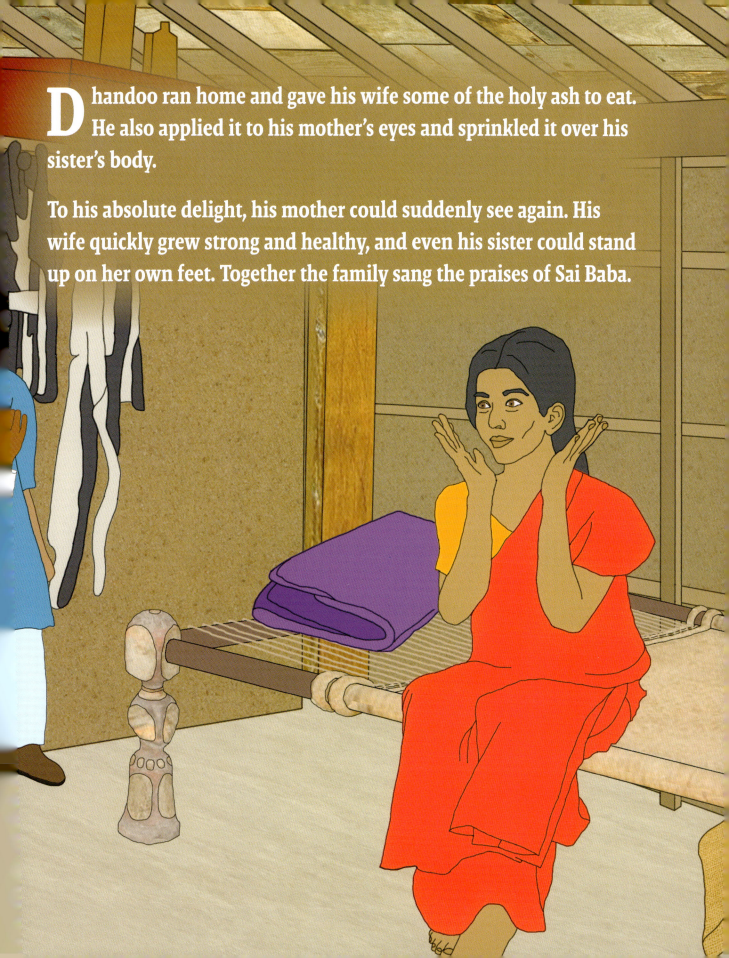

Dhandoo ran home and gave his wife some of the holy ash to eat. He also applied it to his mother's eyes and sprinkled it over his sister's body.

To his absolute delight, his mother could suddenly see again. His wife quickly grew strong and healthy, and even his sister could stand up on her own feet. Together the family sang the praises of Sai Baba.

As more such miracles occurred in Shirdi, the news spread far and wide. Many people were now walking long distances to come see Baba for help with their problems. Because of Baba's tender-hearted care and love, both sickness and crime became scarce in Shirdi and the surrounding areas.

The village priest soon had no sick people to cure and the police had no crimes to solve. Their work dwindled, and their incomes grew smaller and smaller. They could not see what the villagers saw in this remarkable saint. The priest and the police thought Sai Baba was an imposter, and they were determined to prove it to all his believers.

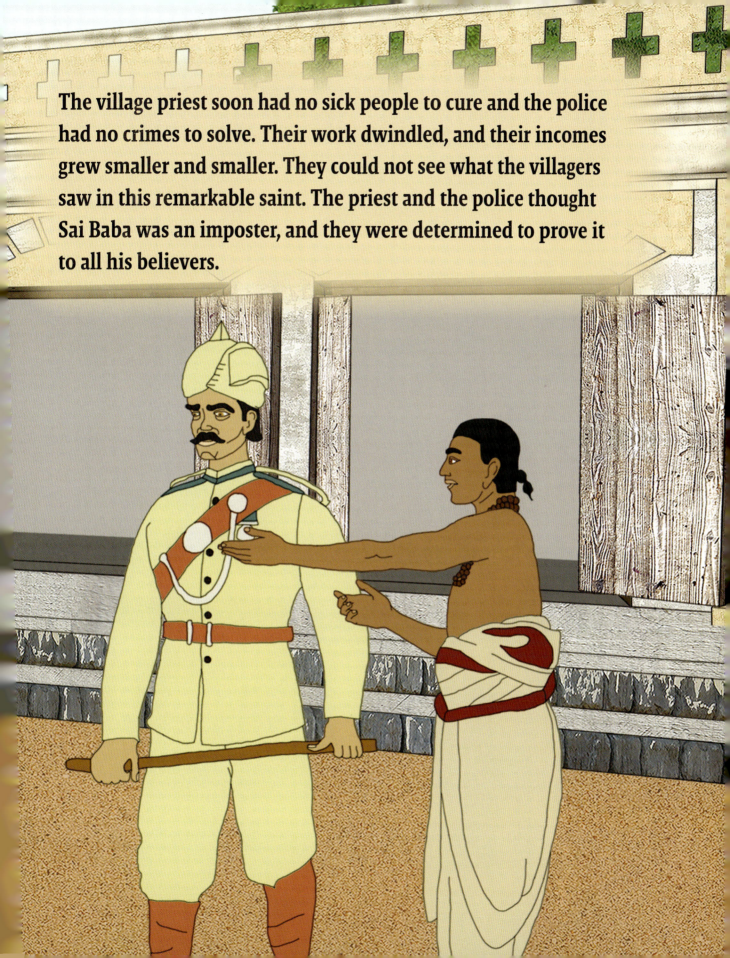

Together they planned an evil scheme. They got hold of a poisonous snake and planned to let it loose on Baba. However, just before they planned to let the snake loose, it turned and viciously bit the priest instead of Baba. The venom quickly ran through the priest's body and he was soon near death.

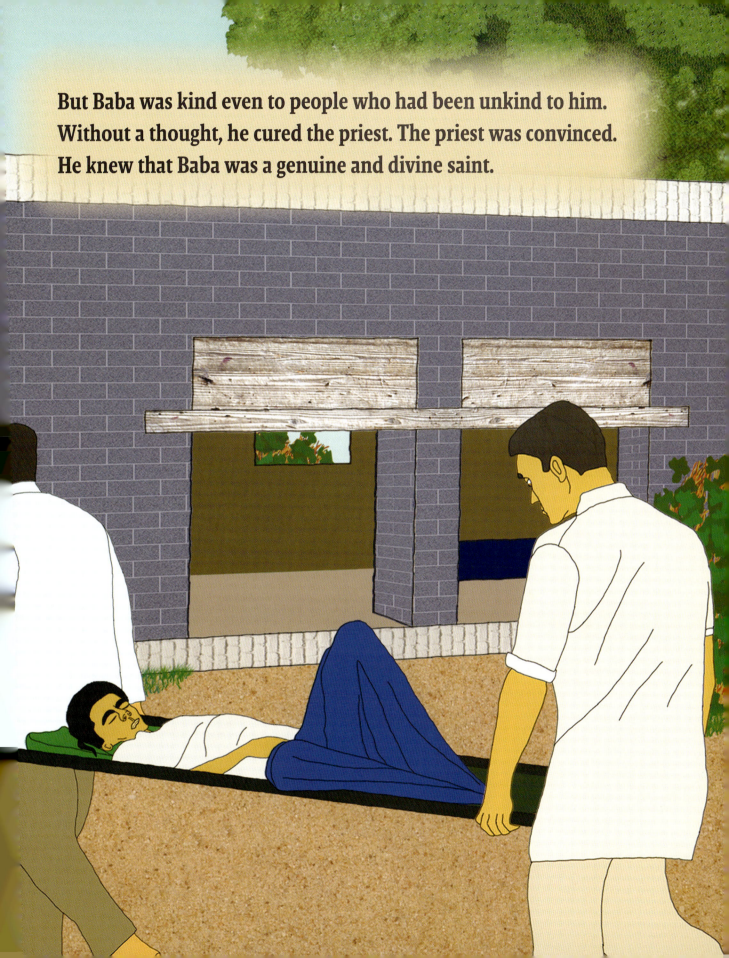

But Baba was kind even to people who had been unkind to him. Without a thought, he cured the priest. The priest was convinced. He knew that Baba was a genuine and divine saint.

When Baba had first arrived in Shirdi, people kept their distance from such a strange-looking man wearing an unfamiliar kind of robe. However, a woman named Bayaji Ma used to give him food every day, sometimes walking for hours in search of Baba. She cared for him like her own son, Tatya. In gratitude, Baba promised her that he would always take care of Tatya.

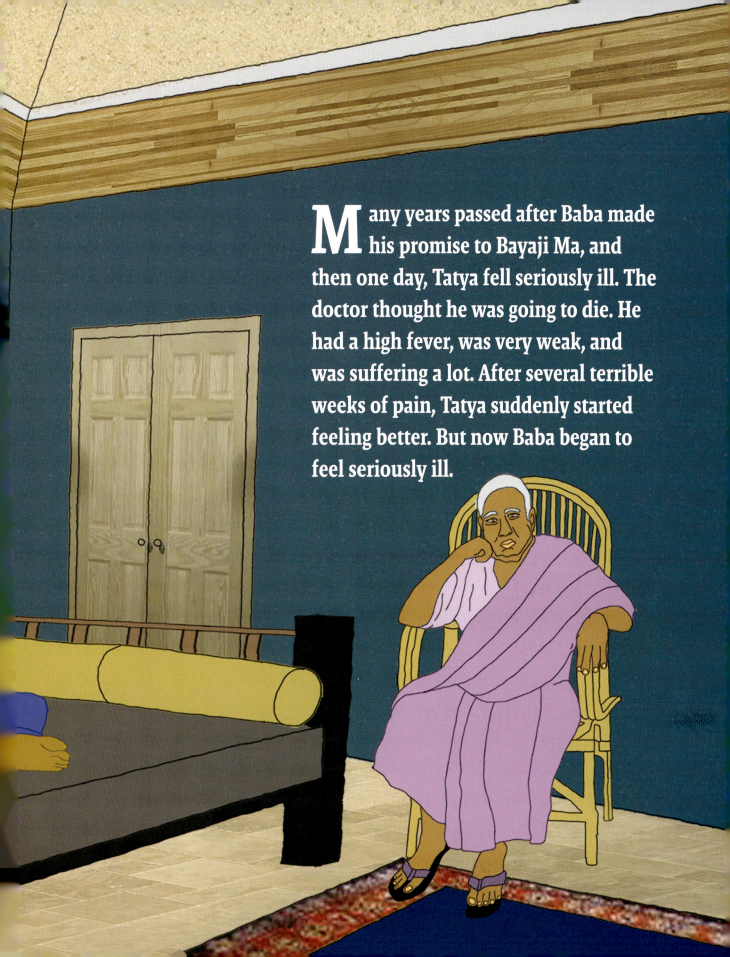

Many years passed after Baba made his promise to Bayaji Ma, and then one day, Tatya fell seriously ill. The doctor thought he was going to die. He had a high fever, was very weak, and was suffering a lot. After several terrible weeks of pain, Tatya suddenly started feeling better. But now Baba began to feel seriously ill.

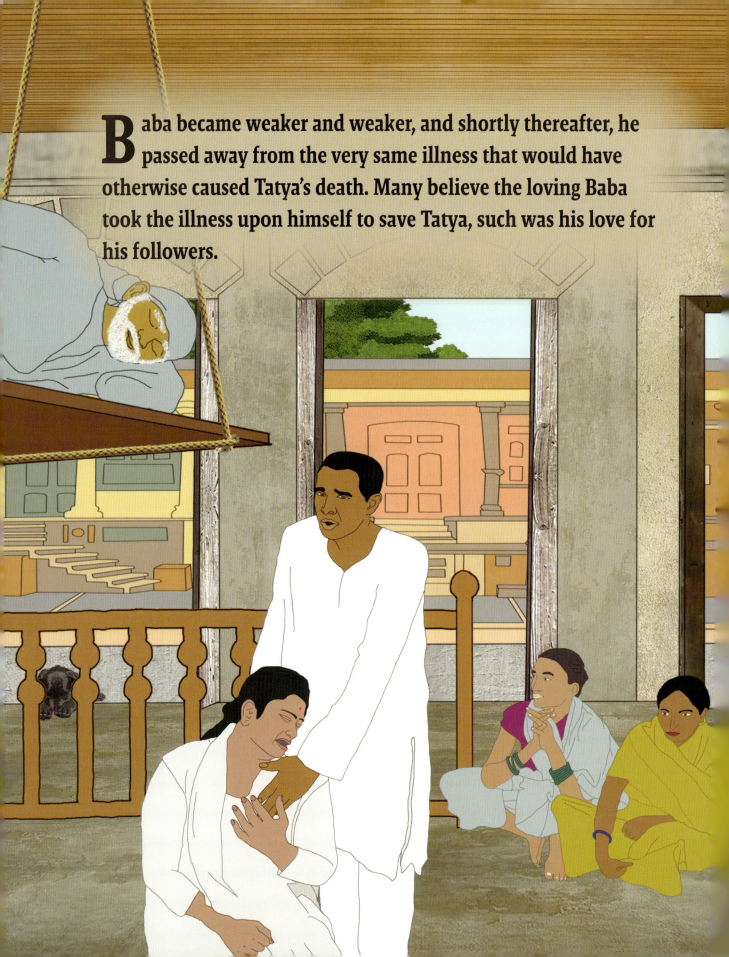

Baba became weaker and weaker, and shortly thereafter, he passed away from the very same illness that would have otherwise caused Tatya's death. Many believe the loving Baba took the illness upon himself to save Tatya, such was his love for his followers.

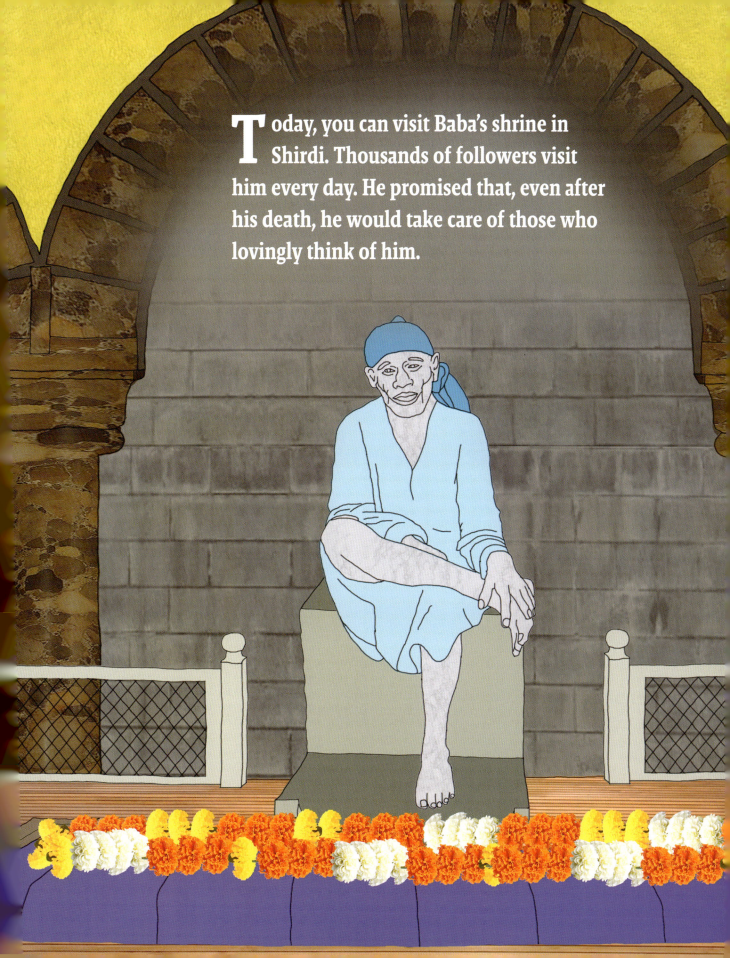

Today, you can visit Baba's shrine in Shirdi. Thousands of followers visit him every day. He promised that, even after his death, he would take care of those who lovingly think of him.

Love Heals...

Pain, anger, hatred, and disease. Sai Baba was a most loving Indian saint (spiritual master). His love was unconditional, and it knew no boundaries. He is not associated with any religion. He always said "Sabka Malik Ek" meaning *Everyone's Master is One.*

Sai Baba was abandoned at birth and had a difficult childhood yet grew up to be an extraordinarily loving person. He dedicated his life to the welfare of others.

Sai Baba's date of birth, his birthplace, and his early life are largely unknown and debatable. Due to a lack of evidence, no definitive information exists to prove what Sai Baba's life was like before he arrived in Shirdi.

Baba reportedly arrived at the village of Shirdi when he was about sixteen years old. Although there is no agreement among biographers about the date of this event, it is generally accepted that Baba stayed in Shirdi for three years.

He left the village and returned later with a marriage party to live in Shirdi for the rest of his life. For four or five years after his arrival in Shirdi, Baba lived under a neem tree and often wandered for long periods in the nearby jungle to meditate.

He adopted his famous style of dressing, consisting of a knee-length one-piece Kafni robe and a cloth cap. His manner was said to be withdrawn and uncommunicative as he undertook long periods of meditation. He was eventually persuaded to take up residence in an old and dilapidated mosque and lived a solitary life there, surviving by begging for alms, and receiving few visitors.

In the mosque he maintained a sacred fire which is referred to as a *Dhuni*, from which he gave sacred ash (*Udi*) to his guests before they left. The ash was believed to have healing and apotropaic powers. He performed the function of a local physician or wise man known as a *Hakim* and treated the sick by application of ashes.

Sai Baba opposed all persecution based on religion or caste. He was an opponent of religious orthodoxy. He advised his devotees and followers to lead a moral life, help others, love every living being without any discrimination, and develop two important features of character: devotion to the Guru (*Sraddha*) and waiting cheerfully with patience and love (*Saburi*).

In his teachings, Sai Baba emphasized the importance of performing one's duties without attachment to earthly matters and being content regardless of the situation. Sai Baba encouraged charity and stressed the importance of sharing.

About the Author

Arthi Gokarn loves children and art. Her own struggle with alopecia universalis made her realize how easy it is to lose hope and become bitter amid adversities. Getting through it requires love, support, faith, and the hope for a miracle.

During this period, she also became aware of the struggles of foster children and has been inspired to help them by illustrating the true story of the life of a foster child that involves abandonment, pain, love, hope, healing, and miracles. This is her first attempt at creating a book. She hopes that the story of Sai Baba touches the lives of children who need it the most.

About the Illustrator

David Flenniken is a passionate creator and highly energetic individual. From technical engineering diagrams to portraits to children's books, he pays attention to the details that both catch the eye and touch the heart.

This project grew out of his previous well-received Tarot card project, which has been a local success. He only works on projects that he feels called to participate in and this project is one of them. He hopes that the reader is touched as much as he was by the story and energy of Sai Baba.